ISBN 0-86163-462-4

This edition first published 1990 by
Award Publications Limited,
Spring House, Spring Place,
Kentish Town, London NW5 3BH

Printed in Germany

THE
WILD WOOD

from Kenneth Grahame's
THE WIND IN THE WILLOWS

Adapted by Jane Carruth

Illustrated by Rene Cloke

AWARD PUBLICATIONS

There were times, after a day on the river, when Ratty would talk about his friends, especially Toad and the Badger.

"I know Mr. Toad, of course!" Mole said, as they talked one evening. "But I don't know Mr. Badger…"

"Badger lives in the Wild Wood," Ratty said. "We certainly don't want to go visiting him there!"

But Mole couldn't stop thinking about Badger and, one morning, when Ratty had gone fishing, he set out for the Wild Wood.

It was a cold and wintry day and Mole, in high spirits, was glad of his warm scarf. Once inside the wood, however, his spirits fell for it seemed the place was full of little pointed faces watching him. Suddenly a big rabbit sped past muttering, "Danger, danger, everywhere! Get out!"

"What danger?" Mole asked himself, all at once very much afraid.

Meanwhile Ratty had come home. He did not
miss his friend for some time but as the day wore
on he grew anxious.

"Where can he be?" he asked himself over and
over again.

It was only when he went to look outside that he
was suddenly aware, for the first time, of Mole's
tracks.

"I do believe he has set out for the Wild Wood
after all!" he exclaimed in dismay. "What a
foolish, foolish Mole!"

Rat was too stout-hearted to desert his friend.
He went back into the house, put on his warmest
clothes and armed himself to the teeth. Then he set
out for the Wild Wood.

Once in the Wild Wood Ratty began his search. Up and down he tramped, sometimes calling in a soft voice, "Moly, Moly where are you?"

Every now and then Rat caught glimpses of evil little faces peering at him from behind trees but he kept on bravely. And, at last, after an hour's search, he heard a feeble little cry, "Is that you Ratty? I'm here!"

The cry came from a hollow at the foot of one of the trees and Ratty bent down and looked inside. There was Mole, shivering and shaking and looking so scared that Ratty said, "Now pull yourself together, Moly. We must get going out of here…"

"I'm sorry Ratty," Mole whispered, "I can't go yet…I'm so tired and now that you've found me…I feel like a little sleep." And he put his head down and to Ratty's dismay began to snore.

It was snowing hard when Mole was fit enough to walk and it was only by the greatest good luck that Ratty found the doormat and Mole tripped over the door-scraper and hurt his leg!

"Never mind your leg!" Ratty exclaimed
unkindly. "This doormat and that scraper you're
sitting on tell me that somewhere under this bank
of snow is Badger's house!"

Rat and Mole set to work on the snow bank and
presently they came upon a solid little green door
and beside it a brass plate which read
MR. BADGER.

"You hang on to the bell-pull," Rat said, "and
I'll hammer on the door."

Mole swung on the
bell-pull while Ratty
hammered on the door.
After a time there was a
slow shuffling sound.
Then the noise of a bolt
being drawn. The door
opened and there was
old Mr. Badger, a
lighted candle in his
hand.

"Do let us in,
Badger," Ratty cried.
"We're lost and it's so
cold…"

"Come in both of you," said Badger in a deep
kindly voice. "The kitchen is the place for you and
I've plenty of food!"

Badger found them
dressing-gowns and
slippers and sat them
down at a table laden
with delicious food.

"Made the sausage rolls myself this very
afternoon," said Badger, "and there are plenty of
apples and a very tasty vegetable pie though I do
say so myself!"

Ratty and Mole looked at each other and smiled
The Wild Wood seemed miles away!

13

After a really wonderful supper, the Water Rat
told Mr. Badger how he had come to meet Mole.
And then Mole told Badger how he came to be in
the Wild Wood. "I was looking for you," he said,
smiling.

Mr. Badger looked pleased and when he finally
took Ratty and Mole into his storeroom where he
kept his spare beds, he was particularly gracious to
Mole.

Rat and Mole slept very well and, in the morning when they came into breakfast, they both had good appetites. They shared the meal with two young hedgehogs who had called to see Badger, knowing he would give them a good breakfast.

Otter was another unexpected visitor. "So there you both are!" he cried, bursting into the room. "I tell you we were all worried about you. Some of us searched the river bank…I said I would come here."

Soon after the two hedgehogs had gone home,
Mr. Badger invited Mole, Ratty and Otter to stay to
lunch.

Lunch was very enjoyable and Mole was so
clearly pleased at being with Mr. Badger that the
kindly fellow offered to take Mole all over his
house. Mole was delighted and his new friend lit a
lantern and gave him a conducted tour through

the long dark passages and down the steep walkways which led into a number of different storerooms.

When they got back, Ratty was impatient to be off. "We don't want to be spending another night in the Wild Wood," he said. "Come on, Moly, get your coat on. You can visit Mr. Badger another time."

"I'm coming too," said Otter. "I know this wood. I'll lead the way!"

After their adventure in the Wild Wood, the
weather changed and the snow disappeared. Mole
had been staying with Ratty so long that he
scarcely ever thought of his own home.

There were so many pleasant and exciting things
to do that Mole had very little time to himself to
think about his old life.

But all this was to change. One day he was out
with Ratty. They had been for a very long walk
and been much further than usual. "You know,"
said Mole, stopping suddenly in his tracks,

18

"there is something very familiar about this place. I seem to have been here before." And he sniffed the air. But Ratty paid no attention and strode forward, anxious to be home again...

Mole trotted after his friend. His little face wore such an anxious, troubled look that Ratty couldn't help noticing it when they stopped.

"Sit down here," he said in a kindly way, "and tell me what's wrong."

"It-it's just that something about the place reminds me of home," Mole whispered beginning to sob. "But you w-wouldn't stop..."

"Well now," said Ratty, "what a cruel fellow you must take me for! I'm afraid I was thinking too much about our supper. Cheer up, Mole, we'll turn back at once." And he took Mole's paw.

Mole cheered up as they hurried along. Then he began to sniff the air and look about him with great excitement.

"What is it, old boy?" Ratty asked at last. "Where are we going?"

"Home!" gasped Mole, his little eyes bright. "I do believe I've stumbled on my old home — my own dear home!"

He had scarcely stopped speaking when he took a dive through a hedge. Ratty followed, not without difficulty, and was just in time to see him dart into a tunnel. The tunnel had a queer earthy smell and was very dark. But at the end of it Rat saw that they were standing in an open space.

Mole took a lantern from a nail in the wall and struck a match. And there it was — the front door of his own house!

"There it is," said Mole. "We're home!"

Ratty couldn't help thinking how cold and damp everything was once they were inside but he said nothing. Instead he busied himself collecting bits of wood that were lying around and built a fire.

Mole no longer looked excited but when he saw his friend hard at work making a fire, he began to look more cheerful.

He found a duster and began dusting the chairs and table. "I-I had forgotten how long I have been away," he said as he dusted. "I used to be so proud of my little home. Kept everything neat and tidy..."

"I can see that!" Ratty said kindly. "We'll have the place shipshape in no time at all."

"Of course we will!" said Mole.

But Mole didn't stay cheerful for very long. He began to feel hungry. "We haven't anything for supper, Ratty," he said. "I feel so ashamed…"

"We don't know yet," said Ratty, who was also feeling hungry. "Let's explore the cupboards. You never know!"

To Mole's delight they found quite a few things they could eat. The tins of sardines were excellent, so was the German sausage also in a tin. Then there were the bottles of ginger-pop and the box of dry biscuits.

They had just started on their second tin of sardines when there was the scuffling of small feet outside.

"We've got visitors!" Mole exclaimed. And then came the sound of singing. "I think it must be the carol singers. They always used to come to my house last of all and I would give them hot drinks…"

"Let's have them in!" Ratty cried, and he ran to the door.

The field mice carol singers made a merry sight as they trooped in and formed a circle.

"Now then, boys!" said their conductor, lifting his baton.

Mole didn't seem to enjoy the lovely carols. "I'm sorry Ratty," he whispered at last. "I'm so worried. We haven't a thing to give them…"

Ratty said nothing but presently he spoke to the conductor. "Be a good lad," he said in a low voice. "Take this money and buy as much as you can. Fill the basket with things to eat and drink…"

"There's a shop in the village which stays open all hours," said the conductor. "I'll be as quick as I can, sir!" And he hurried off, swinging the basket.

After the mice had sung one or two of Ratty's favourite carols, he told them all to sit on Mole's big settee — it was a tight squeeze! And there was a lot of pushing and giggling.

There was still enough ginger-pop to fill their mugs and they looked very happy and content, especially when Ratty said that each one could recite his best poem if he wanted to.

By the time two or three of the mice had given recitations, their conductor was back. And my, what a feast they had! Mole's eyes nearly popped out of his head when he saw all the goodies spread out on the table. It was a splendid sight!

After the feast, Mole and Ratty joined in some of the party games, and then it was time for the happy little mice to go home.

Mole and Ratty stood in the doorway to wave them goodbye.

"Goodbye, Goodbye!" they called back. "And thank you again!"

Mole sighed with happiness. "It's all thanks to you, Ratty," he said at last.

The house felt strangely quiet after the carol singers had gone but Mole didn't mind. He sat with Ratty before his very own fire, feeling very content with life.

Ratty understood what Mole was thinking.

"It's like this, old fellow," he said. "East, West, home is best…"

"That's true," said Mole. "But don't imagine I want to live here all the time. If you don't mind, Ratty, I'd just like to come home sometimes…"

"That's settled then," said Ratty, as Mole looked out clean patchwork quilts.

"You'll come home with me tomorrow, but you'll come back here whenever you feel like it."

Mole nodded happily as he climbed into bed. What a wonderful friend Ratty was! And how well the day had turned out after all. And Ratty, as he closed his eyes, was thinking much the same about Mole.

Soon there wasn't a sound to be heard except for Mole's soft little snuffling snores!